# FLYING FURBALLS

# Most Wanted

## DONOVAN BIXLEY

upstart press

*In memory of Sinja, who was too fond of speedy cars.*

The publishers would like to remind all
cat and dog owners that their pets should
not drive or fly without an approved licence
from RATS (Road And Transport Safety).

A catalogue record for this book is available from the
National Library of New Zealand

ISBN 978-1-927262-99-3

An Upstart Press Book
Published in 2017 by Upstart Press Ltd
Level 4, 15 Huron St, Takapuna
Auckland, New Zealand

Text and illustrations © Donovan Bixley 2017
The moral rights of the author have been asserted.

Printed by 1010 Printing International Limited, China

# MEET SOME OF THE
# CHARACTERS AT CATs HQ

**Claude D'Bonair** is the youngest pilot in the CATs Air Corps. He learned to drive and fly as a kit — travelling to exotic countries with his father. He's never afraid to leap into dangerous situations.

**Syd Fishus** was once a handsome pilot with a huge appetite for adventure. Now he has a huge appetite for lobsters and cream — among other bad habits. The only thing he won't eat is stonefish.

**Major Ginger Tom** is the most famous dogfighter in all of katdom, with three bestselling autobiographies: *Cat's in the Cradle with a Silver Spoon*, *Ginger Bred*, and *High as a Kite*.

**C-for** is a brilliant inventor, who went to university in the old dog kingdom. Since the war, he has been forced to hide his collection of music by dog composers like Bark and Woofgang Mozart.

**Manx** is never afraid to say what she thinks. She's always busy taking apart machines and making them better. She's also busy looking after her two sisters.

**Wigglebum** is full of energy and loves playing pranks. **Picklepurr** thinks there's nothing you can't learn from a good book.

**General Fluffington** has a wicked sweet tooth — he even likes sugar on his jellymeat.

**Mr Tiddles** loves to sing when having a cat bath. He secretly dreams of upstaging everyone.

As soon as the war is over, **Commander Katerina Snookums** would like nothing better than a quiet spot of fishing.

**Nurse Mitzi** is the youngest from a large aristocratic family. She wants to be a doctor.

**Nurse Sinja** loves fast cars, and ran away from home to join the Medical Corps.

**Mrs Cushion**'s first name is **Velvet**. Her eyesight is terrible but her hearing is purrfect.

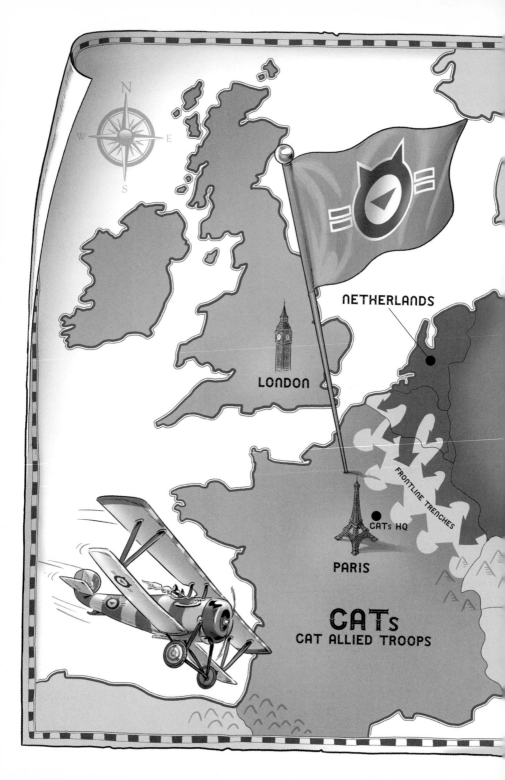

BERLIN

# DOGZ
**DOG OBEDIENCE
GOVERNED ZONE**

# EUROPE 1917

The great war continues. Cats and dogs once lived together in peace. That was before a pack calling themselves DOGZ took over the kingdoms of Central Europe. As the invading DOGZ army conquers more countries, the Cat Allied Troops (CATs) have gathered from every corner of the katdom to save Europe from going to the DOGZ.

# CHATEAU FUR-DE-LYS

CATs headquarters (HQ) on the outskirts of Paris.
The chateau and beautiful gardens were the setting
for the famous novel *The Three Mouseketeers*.

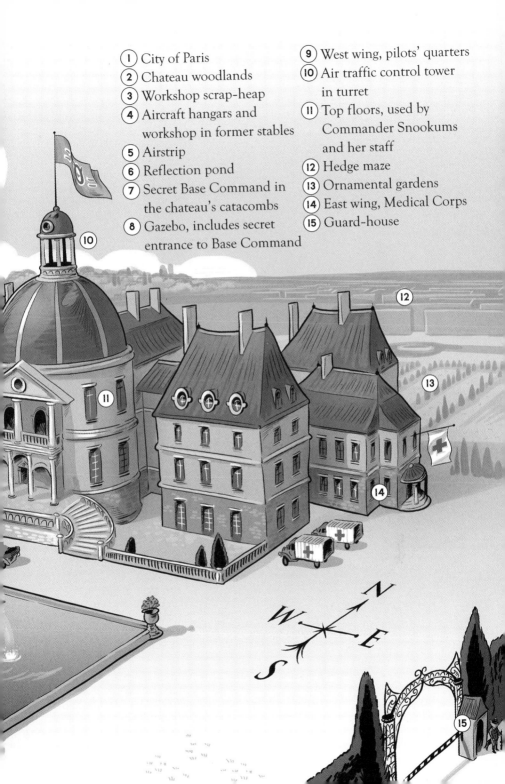

1. City of Paris
2. Chateau woodlands
3. Workshop scrap-heap
4. Aircraft hangars and workshop in former stables
5. Airstrip
6. Reflection pond
7. Secret Base Command in the chateau's catacombs
8. Gazebo, includes secret entrance to Base Command
9. West wing, pilots' quarters
10. Air traffic control tower in turret
11. Top floors, used by Commander Snookums and her staff
12. Hedge maze
13. Ornamental gardens
14. East wing, Medical Corps
15. Guard-house

# CHAPTER 1

'**S**pying spaniels!' spluttered General Fluffington. 'The DOGZ seem to know our every secret.'

Commander Katerina Snookums wrung her paws. 'They're always one step ahead of us,' she said. 'DOGZ planes are winning victory after victory.'

Claude D'Bonair leapt to his feet. The young daredevil was gaining a reputation as one of the bravest pilots at Cat Allied Troops. 'What about news that some dogs have turned tail and are fighting on our side?' he said.

'Poppycock!' snorted General Fluffington. 'You will learn, young Claude, that there are only two types of dog in this world, those who smell butts, and those whose butts smell.'

'But . . . but . . . but . . .'

'Exactly!' said General Fluffington. He turned his attention to the assembled squadron. 'That's why I've summoned CATs' top dogfighters for our most urgent mission. Have you all read today's newspaper?'

# RED SETTER TOP TERROR

### Fifi Hackles updates us on the most deadly dog in the skie

With his unmistakable red plane, K9, The Red Setter rules the skies. He is an unstoppable enemy and a key reason why the DOGZ army continues to advance on Paris, with victory after victory.

Yesterday, the DOGZ top fighter ace notched up his 43rd victory, downing a CATs bomber near the front lines.

Just mention of The Red Setter's name strikes fear across katdom. A spokesperson from CATs HQ had

this to say about The Red Setter 'I think you'll find he's actually more of a russet-brown colour.'

CONTINUED ON PAGE 11.

FILE PHOTOGRA

---

## TREASURES OF EGYPT

Musée du Louvre, Paris.
Showing daily 9am – 7.30pm

*bring your mummy to see our mummies*

## CATPRONI PLANE IN PRODUCTION

A new aeroplane design by Catproni has gone into production this week, after the plans were obtained in a daring undercover mission by CATs agents in Venice. The new aircraft will be the best

## ROYAL ESCAPE

King Charles Spanie is on the run, havin escaped from the DOGZ' clutches.

His whereabouts a unknown, and the remaining Dog Ro are still being held captive by Alf Alp Many believe the former King of th

ur cartoonists give us something to laugh about.

BY REX

**E LIGHTER SIDE OF THIS WEEK'S HEADLINES**

Alf Alpha marks out DOGZ new territory

## Puss in Bootcamp

## Major Paine

Captain Syd Fishus chortled as he read the paper. It was hard to believe that Claude's old friend had once kept himself in all-round good shape — now he *was* an *all-round* shape! 'Wee gains,' Syd laughed at the cartoon.

'I'm not talking about the funny pages!' bellowed General Fluffington.

'I'm talking about The Red Setter. This newspaper makes us look like we're as helpless as a kitten up a tree. If this K9 menace is allowed to rule the skies we'll all be in enemy kennels eating dog roll before you can say "sizzling sardines".'

At that moment, Mr Tiddles, the General's secretary, came in, happily humming a tune.

He stopped abruptly when he saw the pilots — as if he'd been caught doing something bad. He placed a huge stack of documents on the desk.

'Perfect timing,' said General Fluffington, thumping the pile of documents with his fist. 'Mr Tiddles has access to all our top-secret files. He has prepared this 137-page report on how to capture The Red Setter. I want you all to take a copy and read it thoroughly.'

The entire squadron let out a combined groan. Mr Tiddles' reports were as enjoyable as an infestation of fleas.

'The Red Setter is our *most wanted* enemy,' the General continued. 'Therefore, I'm ordering double patrols, day and night. I want you to live in your planes, eat in your planes, sleep in your planes . . .'

'Sleep in our planes?' queried Claude.

'Well, maybe it would be best if the pilots didn't sleep in their planes,' said Commander Snookums.

'Won't eating in our planes make a mess in them?' piped up another pilot.

'Well . . . I . . . um,' stumbled the General. 'That was more of a suggestion.'

'And what if we need to use the sand box?' added Syd with a smirk.

'Well, no . . . we *definitely* can't have *that* in a plane.'

'And what about . . .'

'Enough!' boomed the General. 'I want that mangy Red Setter brought to heel! No more tom-foolery.'

Just then, Major Ginger Tom entered the room.

'Sorry I'm late, chums,' said Major Tom, grabbing

a cup from Mrs Cushion's tea trolley. Everyone was surprised to see CATs' most famous dogfighter at the briefing. He was usually too busy on some unbelievably dangerous mission, or at least writing about some unbelievably dangerous mission, like the part in Major Tom's autobiography when he leapt from his burning plane into the cockpit of an enemy fighter, knocked the pilot unconscious and flew back to base with the dog as a prisoner.

High as a Kite, the Major Tom Story Volume 3

"I subdue the enemy."

'What have I missed?' asked Major Tom.

'It's The Red Setter,' said Commander Snookums. 'He eludes our every patrol. It's as if he has a spy right here at CATs HQ.'

'Codswallop!' said Major Tom. 'Obviously The Red Setter's just too afraid to face *me*. Tell you what, chums, I'll lead the entire squadron, and we'll soon put an end to this nonsense.'

'You'll need to read my report,' said Mr Tiddles, handing the Major a stack of papers.

Major Tom snorted at the idea. 'Boring reports may be fine for you desk pilots, but I'm a hot-blooded dogfighter. I'm here to drink cream and whip DOGZ butts . . .' Major Tom peered into Mrs Cushion's cream jug, '. . . and we're all out of cream. That leaves only one thing to do. Who's with me?' he cheered.

A fat bumblebee meandered across the airfield, bobbing lazily from flower to flower. Claude yawned and stretched out in his sun chair. It had been days since General Fluffington's orders. Still there'd been no sign of The Red Setter. Claude was sitting beside an unfortunately named Sopworth Pup — a standard fighter from the CATs air fleet. But it wasn't the same as his beloved Kitty Hawk — *that* plane had been shot down by the infamous red pooch.

Lookouts had been posted along the entire battle front. If The Red Setter did show up, a siren would sound and Claude's squadron would swarm like bees protecting the hive against a pesky wasp. But so far there had only been false alarms. All this waiting around left Claude's imagination to run wild.

He kept thinking over what Commander Snookums had said — there was a DOGZ spy at CATs HQ. At that moment, Claude spotted Mr Tiddles across the airstrip, acting very suspiciously. The General's secretary came out of the Chateau and glanced around nervously before sneaking along the side of the building. Claude noticed that Mr Tiddles had a pile of papers tucked under his arm.

*What's going on here?* Claude wondered.

He was about to follow Mr Tiddles when the roar of an engine blasted across the field.

Claude leapt to his feet, expecting an attack from above. Instead, he saw Syd's convertible charging down the airstrip. But something was very wrong. The car veered wildly to the left, narrowly missing a row of fighter planes, then it swung back to the right.

Pilots scattered from their sun chairs. Claude threw up his arms as Syd's car came zooming straight at him. At the last second, the car screeched to a halt in a spray of dirt and grass.

Syd was in the front seat. His teeth were clenched and his eyes had a terrified gleam. Beside Syd, in the driver's position, sat Nurse Sinja with a beaming smile plastered across her face.

'Crikey dingo!' swore Syd. 'I crossed the Australian desert with Claude's dad and a car full of deadly stonefish, but that wasn't half as scary as driving with Sinja.'

Sinja patted Syd's arm. 'Syd's always exaggerating,' she purred. 'He's teaching me to drive.

I'm applying to be a Mobile Medical Kit in the
Ambulance Corps.'

'What a great ambition,' said Claude. 'We need
more Mobile Medical Kits.'

'We will do if Sinja's behind the wheel,' said Syd.

'Oh, Syd's such a joker,' giggled Sinja. 'But
underneath he's a real sweetie — aren't chew, Syd?'
She grabbed Syd's cheek and gave it a waggle.
'You're just a gwreat bwig softie. Now off we go.' She
clunked the gearstick forward.

'Smoothly does it,' winced Syd, patting his
precious car. There was a grinding of gears as the
car jolted off. Claude laughed to himself as the car
bunny-hopped around the reflection pond.
Syd loved that car almost as much as
Claude loved Kitty Hawk. 'I suppose
that's all the excitement I'll get today,'
Claude said to himself, but he
couldn't have been more wrong.

Two little kittens came rushing from behind. They almost knocked Claude from his feet as they grabbed him about the legs. It was Wigglebum and Picklepurr.

'Come quick, come quick,' called Pickle, tugging on Claude's flying jacket.

'Manx rwealy needs you,' Wiggle insisted.

Claude hurried behind as they led him to CATs' main workshop hangar. What could have happened to his friend Manx?

When they reached the hangar, Manx emerged from the darkness, stepping into the sunshine. She seemed perfectly fine to Claude — except for the loopy grin on her face. Claude wondered what the fuss had been about, until Manx stepped aside. Claude's eyes adjusted to the darkness, and he saw what was behind her.

'Surprise!' said Manx, with a sweep of her arm. 'It took a lot of time and effort. But I've finally finished rebuilding Kitty Hawk.'

# KITTY HAWK
## MODIFIED NIEUPORT 27

(1) Ailerons on each wing help roll the plane to the left or right. Manx has added extra ailerons to the bottom wings for increased manoeuvrability

(2) Tail rudder steers the plane left and right

(3) Tail elevators steer the plane up and down

(4) Fuel tank

(5) Vickers machine gun fires 500 rounds (bullets) per minute. It is one of the most reliable guns and is synchronised with the propeller shaft, so bullets don't hit the propeller blade

(6) 130 horsepower Le Rhône rotary engine, produces top speed of 200 km/hr

(7) Manx's booster — an experimental turbo supercharger, injects more air and fuel into the engine, increasing top speed to 240 km/hr for a limited time

(8) 37-mm cannon in propeller shaft

(9) Pilot's cockpit and controls (see inset)

(10) Fuselage and struts are strengthened to withstand increased engine power

(11) Booster air intake

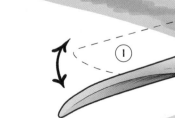

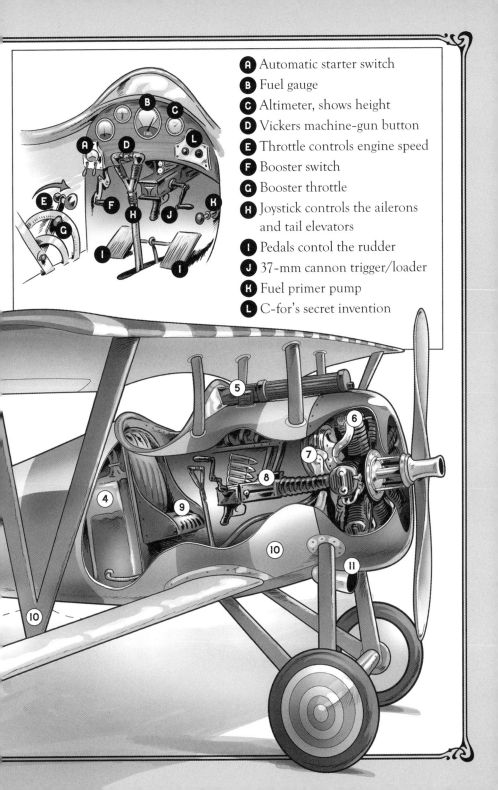

**A** Automatic starter switch
**B** Fuel gauge
**C** Altimeter, shows height
**D** Vickers machine-gun button
**E** Throttle controls engine speed
**F** Booster switch
**G** Booster throttle
**H** Joystick controls the ailerons and tail elevators
**I** Pedals contol the rudder
**J** 37-mm cannon trigger/loader
**K** Fuel primer pump
**L** C-for's secret invention

Claude was gobsmacked.
'You've done a beautiful job,' he
grinned. 'She looks brand new.'

'Better than new,' said Manx.
'Let me show you.' She led Claude
towards the plane. 'I've changed the angle
of the wings, so she's highly manoeuvrable. I've also
strengthened the framework so she can handle all
your wild hi-jinks without breaking apart . . . and
you'll need it. Because I've completely redesigned
the motor.' She patted the engine cowling proudly.
'With my new booster engine, this baby is much
more powerful than anything flying today.'

'Impressive,' said Claude, stroking the glossy
fuselage.

'But I need to warn you,' said Manx,
'this new engine comes at a price. With the
booster at full power, she uses twice as much
fuel as normal.'

Wiggle and Pickle were running around
excitedly. 'What about the paint job,

do you like our new colour scheme?'

Claude stood back and took in the whole aircraft. 'Yellow and black stripes. Now Kitty Hawk looks like a harmless bumblebee,' he said.

'Not harmless,' said Wiggle bouncing up and down. 'Show him, Manx, show him.'

Claude gave Manx a puzzled look. 'Show me what?'

'Okay, okay, calm down you two.' She brought Claude back to the front of the plane. 'Kitty Hawk's got a *real* stinger now.' She tapped the propeller. 'Along with the normal machine gun, I've installed a 37-mm cannon in the propeller shaft. It's enough firepower to punch a hole in a brick wall.'

'I can't wait to take her for a blast,' said Claude.

'As long as you don't blast her apart,' said Manx.

'What do you mean?' said Claude.

Manx cocked an eyebrow at her daredevil friend. 'You don't exactly have the best reputation for looking after aircraft.' She counted them off on her fingers. 'There was my Morane-Saulnier, which never made it home . . .'

'Yes, well . . .'

'. . . and then the Breguet you crashed in the Swiss Alps . . .'

'But that was . . .'

'And remember that DOGZ Pfalz fighter you crashed into a tree?'

'Syd crashed that one,' corrected Claude.

'. . . and what about C-for's Curtiss floatplane?'

'I parked it in the river Seine, just outside CATs' boat sheds.'

'You parked it at the *bottom* of the river,' replied Manx.

Claude gave an embarrassed shrug. 'I forgot
to screw in the bung-hole plug. I didn't know it
would sink!'

'Just try and bring Kitty Hawk back in one piece!'
said Manx.

Claude just laughed and ran his paw along the
wing. 'She's a beauty, Manx. I won't let *anything*
happen to her.' With a graceful pounce, he leapt
into the pilot's catpit.

'Yeahhhaah!' he yelped in horror.

There was a body slumped in the pilot's seat!

For a second, Claude thought it was dead.
Luckily it was only CATs' eccentric
old inventor, C-for, snoring quietly.
Claude tapped him on the shoulder.

C-for woke with a start.
'. . . strangling a cat?
I'm playing the violin!'

'Actually, you were just
having a catnap,' Claude said
gently. 'Sounded like a bad dream.'

'Ah, dreams,' smiled C-for. 'It all came to me
in a dream. Everything was foggy and smoky and I
couldn't see a thing. So that's why I've installed my
latest device in your plane.'

'Does Manx know about this?' asked Claude with
a worried frown.

'Yes, I find six haddock will do the trick,' said
C-for. 'But I don't see what that's got to do with my
invention. This gets you out of trouble every time.
Just press the button and you'll see.'

But Claude *didn't* see. Knowing C-for, this new

device could make the wings fall off — or worse.
C-for eased himself out of the catpit, and showed
Claude the new control he'd rigged into the
instrument panel.

'What *exactly* does it do?' asked Claude,
but C-for didn't have a chance to explain.

A siren blared across the airfield.

*Mee-ow. Mee-ow.*

A voice crackled over the loudspeakers. 'All
pilots, scramble, scramble! The Red Setter has been
spotted. To your fighters immediately.'

There was no time to lose. Claude clambered
into the pilot's seat. The exhausts spat fire as the
powerful new engine roared into life.

Kitty Hawk emerged from the hangar like a bee from a hive. Already the air was abuzz with fighters, taking to the sky in groups — their wheels lifting off the grass as they zoomed past.

C-for hurried behind as Kitty Hawk rolled onto the airstrip. 'I've left some instructions,' he called, waving his walking stick. 'Whatever you do, don't press the button that's coloured—'

But Claude couldn't hear above the drone of engines. He didn't know it yet, but he was headed for the most dangerous dogfight of his life.

# CHAPTER 3

The squadron flew in a wide V formation. Syd Fishus was at Claude's side, bursting out of his catpit like an overstuffed toy — but Claude couldn't want for a better wingman. Leading the formation was Major Ginger Tom. After all the stories Claude had read in Major Tom's autobiography, he was keen to see the famous dogfighter in action.

They'd been flying for only a matter of minutes when Claude spotted a flash of red against the white storm clouds. It *had* to be The Red Setter's distinctive triplane. Major Tom had led them right to their target.

The Major gave a signal and the entire squadron swept around gracefully, as if it were one solid wing. For a moment, Claude thought The Red Setter was going to take them on. Then the red plane banked sharply and headed northwards.

The chase was on!

Huge thunderheads towered on either side — beautiful in the sunlight — but far below, the ground battle was being fought in shadow and storm. They flew straight over the front lines. The Red Setter was making a dash for DOGZ territory.

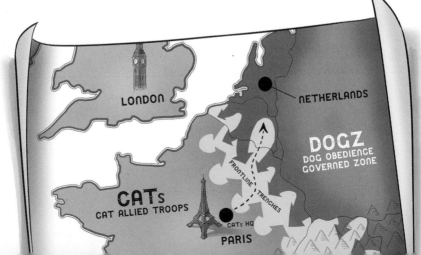

Major Tom led the squadron on and on. But no matter how far they flew, they just couldn't make any gains on the red plane.

'Enough pussyfooting around,' said Claude. He may have been breaking ranks, but he couldn't let The Red Setter get away. He switched on the booster motor. Kitty Hawk's engine gave a high-pitched whine as it ramped into overdrive. Within seconds, Claude had shot ahead of the squadron and was closing on The Red Setter.

Thunder rumbled in the clouds, but there was no lightning. In these conditions it was hard to tell how far the planes had come. It was dangerous to fly into enemy territory. To be shot down here would mean certain capture. But it would be worth the risk if Claude could bring down The Red Setter.

Claude was far ahead of his own squadron now, close enough to see his old foe hunched over the controls, except this time Kitty Hawk was the superior plane and Claude was in the winning position . . . at least that's what Claude thought, until The Red Setter turned and looked back over his shoulder.

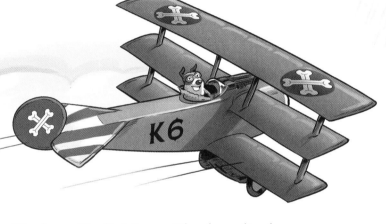

*That's not The Red Setter*, Claude realised.

*What on earth's going on?*

At that instant, thunder burst above.

Not thunder — the roar of engines!

That's what Claude had been hearing.

It was an ambush!

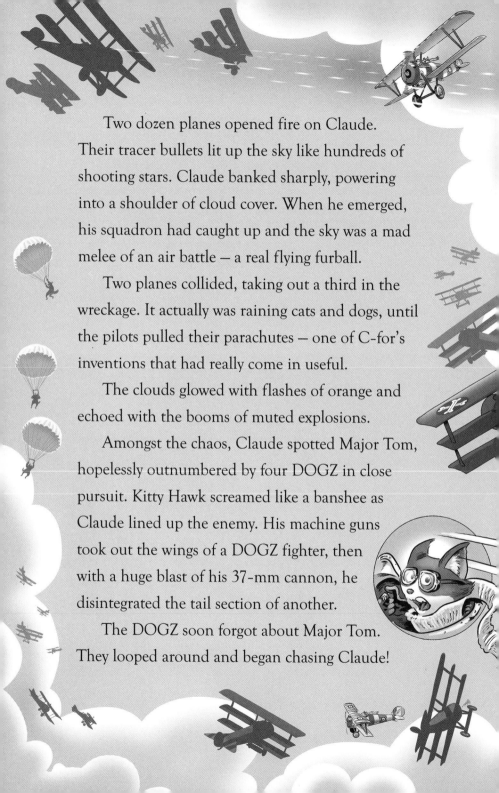

Two dozen planes opened fire on Claude. Their tracer bullets lit up the sky like hundreds of shooting stars. Claude banked sharply, powering into a shoulder of cloud cover. When he emerged, his squadron had caught up and the sky was a mad melee of an air battle — a real flying furball.

Two planes collided, taking out a third in the wreckage. It actually was raining cats and dogs, until the pilots pulled their parachutes — one of C-for's inventions that had really come in useful.

The clouds glowed with flashes of orange and echoed with the booms of muted explosions.

Amongst the chaos, Claude spotted Major Tom, hopelessly outnumbered by four DOGZ in close pursuit. Kitty Hawk screamed like a banshee as Claude lined up the enemy. His machine guns took out the wings of a DOGZ fighter, then with a huge blast of his 37-mm cannon, he disintegrated the tail section of another.

The DOGZ soon forgot about Major Tom. They looped around and began chasing Claude!

A CATs fighter burst from the clouds. It was Syd! He sped past in the opposite direction yelling, 'Take this, you dirty dingos!' With a blast of machine guns, Syd took out one of the DOGZ.

Claude still needed to shake the last fighter. He dived into thick cloud. He couldn't see a thing, then, checking his instruments, he saw the altimeter dropping like a stone.

He was about to hit the ground!

A humungous propeller loomed out of the grey. Claude flicked the joystick, narrowly avoiding collision. *What was this? Some gigantic new DOGZ aircraft?*

KAK
KAK
KAK
KAK
KAK
KAK

*Not propellers*, Claude realised. *Windmills.*

Manx's new controls were superb. Claude jinked right and left as he wove in and out of the twirling blades. The fourth DOGZ fighter was not so skilled. One of the huge fans caught its wing. The fighter exploded with a terrible flash and a thunderclap boom.

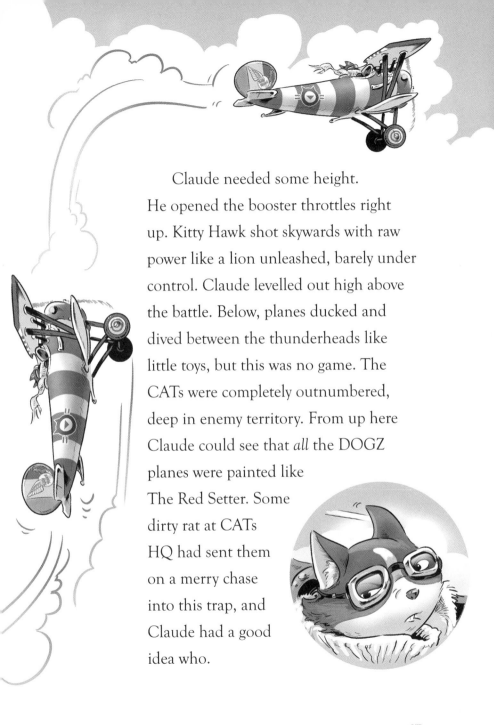

Claude needed some height. He opened the booster throttles right up. Kitty Hawk shot skywards with raw power like a lion unleashed, barely under control. Claude levelled out high above the battle. Below, planes ducked and dived between the thunderheads like little toys, but this was no game. The CATs were completely outnumbered, deep in enemy territory. From up here Claude could see that *all* the DOGZ planes were painted like The Red Setter. Some dirty rat at CATs HQ had sent them on a merry chase into this trap, and Claude had a good idea who.

Claude was ready to charge
back into the battle when he
spotted Major Tom, flying
in a panic and waving one
arm wildly in a circle. It was
the signal for retreat. Syd
flew into view, and Claude
gave him the thumbs up. His old

friend turned and headed for base. The remaining
squadron were already on their way home.

Claude pulled around to follow, when his engine
blew out with a shuddering whirr.

Claude scanned for damage. The controls were
still working.

The engine coughed out a painful puff of smoke,
then stopped completely.

Then Claude remembered Manx's warning
about the booster engine. *Oh, no!* thought Claude.
He desperately tapped the fuel dial, but the gauge
stayed stubbornly empty.

He'd run out of fuel!

Kitty Hawk quickly lost speed and began falling.

Claude watched helplessly as his squadron disappeared. He had no way to call them back.

Worse still, a pack of DOGZ triplanes had spotted him. He was easy pickings now.

Claude had one last chance. The device C-for had installed. *It will get you out of trouble*, C-for had said. But what did it do? Claude noticed C-for's instructions flapping wildly on a string. This was no time for reading instructions. But which button to push? What had C-for yelled? *Don't press the . . .* Claude closed his eyes and jabbed the red button.

KAK
KAK KAK K
KAK
KAK K
KAK K
KAK K
KAK K

Kitty Hawk disappeared into thick cloud. DOGZ triplanes dived after, with machine guns blazing a rain of fire. When Kitty Hawk emerged, smoke was pouring from the fuselage. Claude was slumped unconscious over the controls. The DOGZ fighters plunged after, ready to finish Claude off. This time it looked as if Claude would lose *all* his nine lives.

# CHAPTER 4

Kitty Hawk spiralled earthwards like a meteor trailing smoke. When the DOGZ saw that Claude was doomed, they broke off their attack and gave chase to the rest of Claude's squadron.

It was only then that Claude dared to peek. He'd only been pretending to be shot. The smoke was actually from C-for's new device. He'd have to thank the old inventor for saving his life.

FROM THE DESK OF C-FOR, DEPARTMENT OF CURIOSITY, CATs HQ

# SMOKE SCREEN

You may notice that a new control panel has been installed in your aeroplane's dashboard. Please read these instructions thoroughly before take-off, to familiarise yourself with usage.

① Red button – start / stop

② Yellow button. Never ever, under any circumstances, press this button!

③ Operation – smoke blocks visibility of chasing fighter, allowing quick escape

WARNING: operation when aircraft is grounded may result in choking hazzard

CONTROL PANEL
[ACTUAL CONTROL PANEL MAY DIFFER IN APPEARANCE]

CATs FIGHTER

SMOKE SCREEN

ENEMY FIGHTER

Claude turned off the smokescreen and grabbed the joystick. He pulled Kitty Hawk level to take her down for a soft landing. Well, he would have done, but the controls weren't responding.

'Flying furballs!' cried Claude. He really *had* been hit!

Beneath the clouds spread fields of brightly coloured tulips, lined with rows of windmills. That view was racing closer at an alarming rate. In the rush to scramble, Claude had forgotten his parachute. He'd have to get low enough to leap clear before he crashed his beloved Kitty Hawk.

Claude clambered out of the catpit. The wind buffeted him wildly as he clung on to the joystick. He patted Kitty Hawk goodbye one last time. Ready to jump, Claude put his foot out on the wing. To his surprise, the aileron shifted under his weight.

Instantly the plane banked to one side. He shifted his boot and the plane rolled the other way.

He was controlling the plane with his foot!

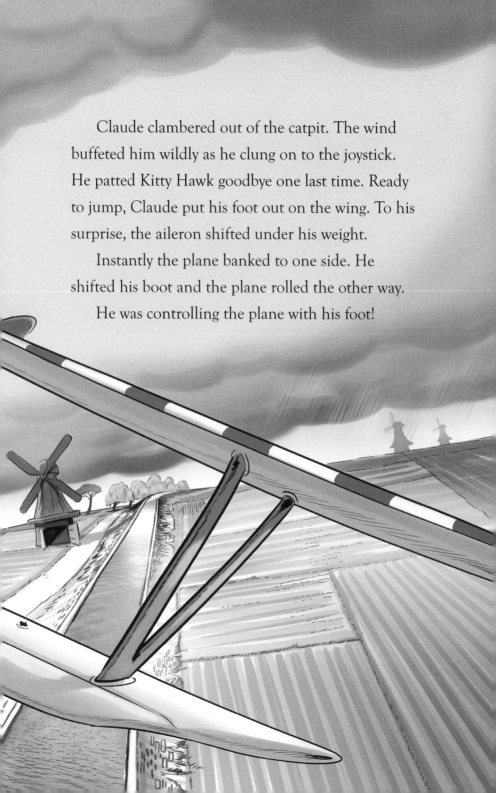

By keeping one paw on the joystick and moving his weight up and down, Claude managed to level Kitty Hawk out.

Between the fields of tulips, he spied a canal banked high with dikes on either side. Running alongside was a stretch of dirt road near a red windmill. Claude aimed for this makeshift landing strip.

Claude came to groggily. He'd been thrown from the
plane's wing when he landed. He felt bruised, but
luckily he'd ploughed into a pile of hay. He hoped
Kitty Hawk had also survived undamaged.

A noise came from the
open doors. A tubby
pup stood watching.
Claude had no idea
how long he'd been
unconscious, or how
long the pup had been
standing there. Suddenly
the puppy dashed off.

'Wait!' cried Claude, leaping to his feet.
He staggered – his head spinning – as the pup
disappeared down the road. Claude had no time to
chase the dog down. For now, he had work to do.

Claude pulled bits of hay from the struts as he ran a quick check over the plane. It hadn't been a pretty landing, but he'd got her down in one piece. As expected, the fuel tank was bone dry — doggone it. There were a few bullet holes in Kitty Hawk's wings, and one lucky shot had snapped the cables that controlled the ailerons.

Claude was no Manx, but he'd learned a bit about fixing planes, travelling as a kit with his dad and Syd on their crazy adventures. He pulled his toolkit from the catpit and set to work.

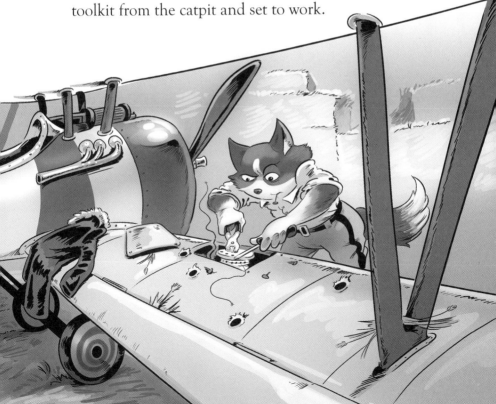

Several times during the
afternoon, he stopped his work,
listening as DOGZ fighters droned
overhead. Claude knew that some of the DOGZ
pilots liked to collect souvenirs from each plane they
shot down. Claude was determined that Kitty Hawk
was not going to be a DOGZ trophy.

Soon enough, Claude had mended the control
cables so they were as good as new. But the repairs
were useless without fuel.

He was putting the covers back on the wing
compartments when he heard a faint rumble.

A cloud of dust rose in the distance.

Claude hauled the doors shut and barred them fast. He dashed to the top of the windmill for a better view. A column of DOGZ army trucks was driving up the road.

As they approached, Claude crept back downstairs. He could only hope that the trucks would pass by the red windmill without stopping . . .

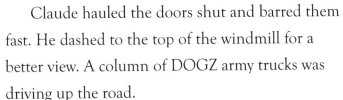

No such luck.

The convoy came to a halt right outside the windmill.

'This is the spot,' called a voice. Soldiers' boots thumped as they jumped down from the trucks.

Claude picked up a pitchfork and waited in silence. He was totally outnumbered, but he wasn't going down without a fight.

Outside, a pack of soldiers approached
the windmill.

'Hey,' asked one of the DOGZ, 'why shouldn't
you play cards with a cat?'

'Cos they're *all* cheetahs,' groaned another
soldier. 'We're sick of your awful cat jokes.'

'Get on with it!' yelled the voice from the truck.
'And make it quick, or the Sergeant will get mad.'

'Sergeant's always mad,' muttered the first dog.

Claude pressed his face to the slits in the door.
He could make out rough shapes surrounding the
building, sniffing and pawing the ground.

Claude stood poised, ready for the soldiers to burst in. Instead, they all raised their hind legs. Claude heard a trickle up against the side of the windmill.

'Are you finished yet?' came the voice from the truck. Claude breathed in relief as the DOGZ relieved themselves. They hopped back into their transport and the convoy moved off.

*Pooh wee*, sighed Claude. *That was too close for comfort.* He needed to stay far away from the DOGZ army and he needed to get some fuel — but where? Fuel tankers weren't just lying around in tulip fields.

The convoy drove off in a trail of dust, and Claude peeked out of the doors.

'Aw, you gotta be kitten me!' he groaned. The last truck in the convoy was a big fuel tanker. To have any chance of escape, he needed to go straight back into the jaws of danger.

# CHAPTER 5

**C**laude found a bike, a farmer's smock and a straw hat in the windmill. He followed the road taken by the convoy. It ran alongside the canal. The countryside stretched out, flat as a tablecloth, as far as the eye could see, decorated with rows of windmills and brightly coloured tulips. A little canal boat chugged past, and Claude pulled his hat down to hide his face.

*I must be in the Netherlands*, thought Claude. In different circumstances, he would have loved to bike through the land of clogs and Edam cheese. But the Netherlands were on the wrong side of the front line. If he was ever going to make it back to CATs territory, Claude needed to find that fuel truck.

As evening came, the sun dropped below the clouds.
Claude crossed a stone bridge as the sunset cast
long shafts of red light across the fields. It looked
spectacular under the dark brooding sky.

In the canal, dragonflies flitted between the
rushes and dipped their wings like little dogfighters,
sending ripples across the water.

As Claude gazed down he suddenly felt very

hungry and sleepy. It seemed as if magical lights began to appear like fireflies reflected in the canal. Looking up, Claude saw it was the lights of a town, coming to life further downstream. From the rooftops fluttered a DOGZ flag.

It was utterly foolhardy to come into a town crawling with DOGZ soldiers, but it was a risk Claude had to take.

Claude left the bike and the farmer's clothes by the canal. Shadows would be his diguise now. He waited until the sun had fully set, then made his way into town. He snuck through the maze of back streets and small lanes. Then followed a side alley, which opened into the main square, where Claude had a good view from the shadows. Sure enough, the DOGZ convoy was there. The trucks were parked outside a tavern. Golden light poured out of the windows and across the cobbles.

If Claude could siphon some petrol from the tanker, he'd be back in Paris for bedtime. Luckily t he DOGZ were all inside making a howling racket. He'd be gone before they even knew he was there. Claude began to sneak across the courtyard when something shocking stopped him in his tracks.

# By order of The Furrer, Alf Alpha
# MOST WANTED
## DEAD OR ALIVE. CLAUDE D'BONAIR

# Reward 100,000 Bones

For: breaking into DOGZ Control Centre, theft of a DOGZ Pfalz aeroplane, destruction of a DOGZ hot air ship, theft of a priceless bottle of whine from The Furrer's private collection.

Claude was frozen at the sight. *HE* was most wanted?! Then, looking around the square, he saw Most Wanted posters glued onto every spare wall.

The DOGZ began leaving the tavern, and were noisily pouring into the square. Claude had missed his opportunity, and that's when he got his second shock.

Limping out of the tavern was Sergeant Wolfgang, the DOGZ commander who had a personal vendetta against Claude. The Sergeant was carrying an armload of Wanted posters. He glued one to the tavern wall as the owner came bustling out.

'Sergeant Wolfgang is after this cat,' said Sergeant Wolfgang.

By order of The Furrer. Alf Alpha
MOST WANTED
DEAD OR ALIVE. CLAUDE D'BONAIR

Reward 100,000 Bones

By order of The Furrer. Alf Alpha
MOST WANTED
DEAD OR ALIVE. CLAUDE D'BONAIR

Reward 100,000

By order of The
MOST W
DEAD OR ALIVE.

Reward 10

'His plane went down near here. He's a menace to all DOGZ, and what's more . . .' the Sergeant looked down at his bandaged leg, '. . . he's responsible for this!'

'Looks like a vicious brute,' said the tavern owner nervously. 'Knowing there's a cat like that around makes my fur stand on end. I've got a wife and pups, you know.' The tavern owner shook with fear and his jowls flapped, spraying spit from side to side. 'Golly me, I'd hate to meet this Claude D'Bonair in a dark alley.'

Across the square, Claude retreated into his dark alley, hoping not to attract attention. He stumbled over a rubbish can, which clattered in the night.

'Look! Over there!' came a yell from the square. 'It's him!'

Claude leapt into the darkness, as boots thundered across the cobbles.

Long shadows chased him down the dark lanes. At every turn he heard barks of, 'This way!' 'After him!'

CLANG

Claude flung himself down a side passage. He ducked under a row of washing, then came to a teetering halt. There stood the tubby little pup from the windmill.

Claude had met many pups on his adventures and they had always been friendly. But with all this propaganda around, he was beginning to see why dogs in this town were so afraid of cats. Could he trust this one?

Shouts came from the distance. Claude glanced nervously at the pup, then put a finger to his lips. 'Shhhhhhh.'

The pup didn't say a word, just looked to the Most Wanted poster, then back to Claude, then back to the poster.

A sudden burst of shouting came from nearby. The DOGZ were close!

The pup sprang into action, grabbing Claude's paw. They headed this way and that with surprising speed, then through a small door, which opened into a little courtyard.

Claude looked around. They'd come to a dead end. Next came the unmistakable smell of dog. Claude's head darted back and forth as shapes emerged from the darkness.

With a sudden rush, his arms were pinned behind his back. Then there was total blackness, as a hood was pulled over Claude's head.

'He's just who we wanted,' said a voice.

'Let's get him to Number One,' said another.

# CHAPTER 6

**W**hen the hood came off, Claude was completely disoriented. The floor seemed to shift and his legs wobbled uneasily as he got his bearings. He was in a narrow room with a low ceiling. Around him were armed guard DOGZ, dressed in a mishmash of uniforms.

'Call Number One,' barked one of the guards. A dog with a face like sagging pancakes rapped on the door at the end of the room. *So this is it,* thought Claude. *I've finally been brought before the terrible Alf Alpha.*

He stood proudly, ready to face the leader who wanted him dead.

But when the door opened it wasn't Alf Alpha. It was someone Claude already knew.

'Rex?' stammered Claude. He'd met the spaniel in Paris. Rex had helped Claude rescue Major Tom. 'What *is* all this?' asked Claude.

'Ever so sorry about the secrecy,' said Rex. 'Welcome to the headquarters of The White Paw.'

'So the rumours are true,' said Claude. 'You're the rebels fighting against the DOGZ army. Where *exactly* am I?'

'A canal boat,' said Rex. That explained the strange wobbling Claude was feeling. 'This way we can move along the canals and keep the DOGZ off our scent.'

Claude followed Rex into the cabin at the front of the canal boat. Comfy chairs faced a woodburner, and a war map was laid out on a large table. A scruffy dog leaned over the map, marking rebel operations. 'Meet Buster,' said Rex, 'my strategic commander.'

'How ya doin', Sunshine?' said Buster.

'And you've already met Gertie.' Rex indicated the tubby pup from the alleyway. 'She doesn't say much, but she's a great scout. Who would ever suspect *her* of being a rebel?'

'So, Sunshine,' said Buster, looking Claude up and down, '*you're* the DOGZ Most Wanted? You could bring a lotta trouble to our secret operation. One hundred thousand bones is enough to turn *any* dog's head.'

'What about all the DOGZ soldiers in the next room?' said Claude.

'They're loyal rebels,' said Rex. 'Members of The White Paw are everywhere, many in the DOGZ army.'

'Why would dogs fight for cats?' said Claude. 'How can I trust any of you?'

'Please,' said Rex, 'let me explain.' They took chairs in front of the stove. 'It's hard to believe, but in the old kingdom I was quite a different dog. I hosted great parties, as my family had done for hundreds of years. We entertained cats and dogs from all over the world. Then Alf Alpha and his DOGZ began stirring up hatred for cats.

'If you so much as had a cat flap on your door, you'd be sent to dog obedience training. Can you imagine, a spaniel like *me* having to "roll over" and "heel" on command like a lap dog?

'The DOGZ started something called "Project Sphinx". They began kit-napping famous cat scientists and engineers to work on their dastardly war machines.

'Many of my friends were cats. As a pure-bred spaniel of the old kingdom, I spoke out against this needless hatred. Soon after, DOGZ soldiers barged into my home with guns and stomping boots.

They stole our family treasures and burned our books. But worse, my family was impounded. By chance, I managed to escape, and here you find me — on the run from my own country.

'We want the same thing, Claude — peace and freedom. The White Paw wants to defeat Alf Alpha and his vision of a world ruled by pure-bred DOGZ. To do that, we need to help each other.'

Claude told them about the DOGZ ambush, how he'd run out of fuel, and how he'd been saved by C-for's smokescreen.

'We heard that the DOGZ were planning to ambush the entire CATs squadron,' said Buster. 'We saw ya plane go down from the canal boat. We couldn't risk coming near because that road is crawling with DOGZ convoys.'

'We sent Gertie to see if you'd survived the crash,' said Rex.

'What I really need is fuel,' said Claude.

'Don't worry about that, Sunshine,' said Buster. 'I'll sort it *all* out. You'll see.'

'For now it's still too dangerous,' said Rex. 'DOGZ are scouring the town for you. But don't worry, we'll get you back to your plane in the morning. In the meantime, you need rest and food.' Rex gave a clap and the door opened. The pancake-faced dog came in and set a plate of cat biscuits and a bowl of double cream in front of Claude.

He hadn't realised just how starving he was.

'Eat up,' said Rex. 'You'll need all your strength to get back to Paris.'

Claude didn't usually drink double cream; it was exactly the kind of thing that made Syd fat and sleepy, but Rex assured him that Holland made the best cream in the world, and a bit of Dutch courage would do him good.

Later Claude felt very alone. Despite Rex's friendly welcome, Claude was deep in enemy territory, and a long way from his friends. Could he *really* trust The White Paw? General Fluffington always said, 'No DOGZ is good dogs'. But Claude was too exhausted to think any more. He curled up on the comfy chair by the fire and was about to drift off when something nudged him from behind. It was Gertie, the little butterball, snuggling into Claude's back. The flickering embers danced across Claude's eyelids, and within seconds he was fast asleep.

**B**y morning The White Paw scouts had returned. Guard DOGZ were patrolling every road and canal in and out of town. Buster drew up an escape plan.

RED
WINDMILL

KITTY
HAWK

TOWN

ROAD

DROP BOMBS
ON ROAD

DIKE

'You need to make your way to the red windmill,' he said. 'You can use the road as an airstrip.'

'What about fuel?' asked Claude.

'Don't fret, Sunshine, it's *all* under control. But The White Paw wants you to do something for us in return.' Buster marked the road. 'This is the DOGZ' main route to and from the front lines. We want it destroyed.'

'How can I do that?' asked Claude.

'Bombs,' grinned Buster. 'You've got a plane, we've got the bombs. Once you take off, just drop the bombs.'

'So how exactly am I supposed to sneak past an army of DOGZ carrying a couple of bombs?' said Claude.

Buster just smiled. 'I've got the perfect disguise, Sunshine.' Buster gave a whistle and Pancake-face came in carrying a traditional Dutch outfit.

'I'm not wearing *that*!' stammered Claude.

Claude felt like an idiot.
But to escape town, the
disguise was necessary, and
the milk containers *were*
a clever way to carry the
bombs. And he *really* did
owe The White Paw for
saving his life. Buster had
been very vague about his
plans, but Claude had to
trust that Rex's strategic
commander would meet
him at the red windmill
with fuel.

Rex guided Claude along back alleyways to the
edge of town, with Gertie running ahead to scout
for trouble. As they passed a big poster of the DOGZ
leader, Rex called, 'Wait!'

'What is it?' said Claude.

Rex pulled out a paintbrush and a small pot of
paint, and made some quick alterations.

'I always find that humour is the best defence,' said Rex, painting a white paw and signing his name.

It suddenly occurred to Claude, 'Are you the *same* Rex who does cartoons for the newspapers?'

'Yes,' chortled Rex. 'At the pala . . . place where I grew up, I had art lessons. As a pup, I was more interested in chasing ducks, truth be told. But my tutor would be pleased to see my art skills being used in defence of the old kingdom.'

Suddenly, Gertie came running, waving her arms frantically.

'Let's get moving,' said Rex.

They snuck to the end of the alley and peeked into the main square. DOGZ trucks were lined up and hundreds of troops were on parade. It was impossible to get through. Then Sergeant Wolfgang appeared. 'Move out! Move out!' called the DOGZ commander. The soldiers leapt into their transports like well-trained pooches. The trucks rumbled into action. Within minutes, the convoy had cleared out of town. Claude's escape was clear. Finally something was going his way.

'Gotta fly,' said Claude. 'Literally,' he laughed. 'It's not safe to hang around this town. That troop convoy could be back at any minute and I want to stay as *far* away from them as possible.'

'Good luck,' said Rex, shaking Claude's paw. 'I'm sure our paths will cross again.'

Gertie grabbed Claude about the legs and gave him a tremendous hug.

There was nothing more Gertie or Rex could do for him now. If Buster had done his job, Claude just had to get back to the red windmill, take off and drop the bombs — then he was home free.

It took Claude a good hour to make it back to the red windmill where he'd hidden Kitty Hawk. He stayed off the main road, keeping to country paths between the trees along the canal. He heard many trucks rumbling up and down the road. That was to be expected on the main highway to the battle front. That was why The White Paw wanted it destroyed. But nothing could have prepared Claude for what he discovered when he came back onto the road.

Dozens of trucks surrounded the windmill, along with hundreds of troops. So *this* was where the DOGZ convoy had raced off to! Even from this distance Claude could make out Sergeant Wolfgang barking orders left and right. In the middle of it all was Claude's beloved Kitty Hawk. The big fuel tanker was parked nearby and DOGZ were refuelling the plane. And there, standing on the wing, as if he owned it, was DOGZ' ace fighter — The Red Setter.

The whole plan was completely kaput now.

Claude quickly turned back towards town. Hopefully, The White Paw had another way to get him home. He'd hardly turned around when coming towards him was yet another truckload of DOGZ soldiers. He was trapped in both directions now!

He put his head down and prayed his disguise would work. The truck rumbled on and the worst Claude got was a few wolf whistles from the soldiers in the back.

He let out a sigh of relief.

Then Claude heard the awful hiss of brakes as the truck came to a halt. He dared not look up as DOGZ boots clumped on the dirty road behind him. His heart juddered against his ribs, desperate to escape like wings inside a cage. But there was no escape now. Dogs had a terrific sense of smell, and if they got any closer . . .

He heard a few sniffs. 'That's strange-smelling milk ya carrying.'

A pair of heavy DOGZ boots appeared in Claude's vision. 'Change of plan, Sunshine,' said the voice.

Claude looked up and found Buster standing before him – wearing a DOGZ commander's uniform! Was this a rescue?

'The DOGZ have upped your reward to half a million bones,' said Buster. 'That kinda money *could* make a dog think twice about where he stands. I'm afraid it's all over, Sunshine.' He turned to the soldiers. 'We have our fugitive!' he barked.

*What? Betrayed!* Buster was crooked as a dog's hind leg.

In an instant, Claude was stripped of his disguise. A soldier went to put shackles on Claude's wrists.

'I'll take care of that,' said Buster, with undisguised glee. He leaned in and whispered something wicked in Claude's ear. Claude frowned, then made a sad face.

Then Claude was marched right into the heart of the DOGZ army. Buster pushed him forward, laughing, 'I'd like to see ya escape now!'

# CHAPTER 8

Buster paraded Claude in front of the DOGZ troops, waving cheerily like some great hero. DOGZ soldiers snarled menacingly, while others cheered and clapped at the capture of DOGZ' Most Wanted enemy.

Sergeant Wolfgang came hobbling through the mob on his broken leg. He looked down on Claude with a terrifying grin. 'Finally!' he growled. 'Sergeant Wolfgang has the famous Claude D'Bonair in his clutches. After that little escape you pulled in Venice, Sergeant Wolfgang's not letting you out of his sight. See this leg? You'll pay for what you did.'

'What shall we do with him, sir?' asked Buster. 'Throw him to the dogs?'

'Sergeant Wolfgang's going to eat 'im,' Sergeant Wolfgang announced to the troops. The soldiers gave a roar of approval.

Claude's eyes sprung wide — was he going

to be eaten alive right here? — until the Sergeant continued. 'That's correct, Sergeant Wolfgang will take the prisoner to the town of Edam. The Furrer, our dear leader Alf Alpha, is visiting Edam. He will be most interested in our little prisoner. This capture is a great morale boost for our troops and a great humiliation to CATs.'

Sergeant Wolfgang was about to order Claude to be loaded into a truck when Buster spoke up.

'I have a way to humiliate CATs even further. Let's get a photograph of DOGZ' Most Wanted enemy for the newspapers.'

'Sergeant Wolfgang agrees,' said Sergeant Wolfgang.

Claude was posed, wrists shackled, in front of his captured plane. On either side stood Sergeant Wolfgang and The Red Setter with their paws on Claude's shoulders.

The DOGZ photographer set up the shot, whilst Buster took great pleasure in directing the scene of Claude's humiliation.

'Make sure the cat is frowning,' he told the photographer. 'Capture his sour and menacing glare.'

*There was no chance of that NOT happening,* scowled Claude.

'Wait,' said Buster. 'How about another photograph of our two arch rivals? *Just* Claude and The Red Setter.'

The photographer captured the scene.

'Darned shame we didn't get to fight it out like cats and dogs in a glorious air battle,' said The Red Setter.

'Still . . . this marvellous aircraft will make a stunning addition to my personal trophies.'

Claude ground his teeth, while Buster kept up the chatter, '. . . and while we're here, let's get one more photo of the captured CATs pilot alone on the wing of his plane?'

'For dogs' sake,' snarled Sergeant Wolfgang. 'Next you'll want him sitting in the cockpit!'

'Great idea!' said Buster. 'It's just for the records. It's not as if he can *escape*. He *is* surrounded by DOGZ troops, and I *personally* shackled his wrists.'

Claude was placed in the cockpit. While the photographer snapped shots, Buster leapt about saying, 'Now look daring; now look menacing.'

Buster was clearly enjoying this. 'Now look like you're about to rain fire and *smoke* on the DOGZ troops.'

*That was the signal!*

*Smoke* was the secret word Buster had whispered in Claude's ear when he'd *pretended* to shackle Claude's wrists. He'd had to change plans when he discovered the DOGZ convoy had beaten him to the windmill.

Claude flicked on C-for's invention. It was designed to leave a pall of smoke behind a speeding aircraft. Here, sitting on the road, thick billows began pouring from the plane, smothering the ground in choking clouds.

Now it was Buster's part to stir up the chaos.
'Fire! Fire!' he yelped, running through the troops.
'Take cover! The fuel truck's gonna explode!'

A mad panic gripped the DOGZ soldiers as they
fled in all directions. Claude made a good show of
looking helpless, crying, 'Save me!' — which no one
tried to do, because he was just a worthless cat.

Within moments Kitty Hawk was completely
engulfed in smoke. Sergeant Wolfgang and
The Red Setter cowered behind one of the trucks.

The DOGZ expected the roar of an explosion at any second. Instead, they heard the plane roaring into life. With a swirl of smoke, the clouds parted. Suddenly they realised it was an escape.

'My trophy!' wailed The Red Setter.

'Sergeant Wolfgang's prisoner!' howled Sergeant Wolfgang. 'Stop him!'

Claude flung his shackles aside and pushed the throttle. Kitty Hawk powered out of the smoke, but the road was blocked by DOGZ trucks.

A couple of soldiers grabbed on to the wings and were edging their way towards Claude. He spun the plane in a sharp turn, sending the dogs sprawling into the tulips.

Now he was heading straight back into the thick of it all, with even less room to take off. On one side rose the dike and on the other the red windmill. All around were soldiers trying to grab hold of the plane. Blocking the road was the fuel truck. He was completely trapped . . . unless . . .

Claude cocked the big 37-mm cannon in the propeller shaft. As the plane swung around, the fuel tanker came into line.

He let rip with the big gun.

The tanker exploded in sheets of orange flame, clearing the way for Claude. The blast was so massive it shook the very foundations of the dike. Water began fizzing out of cracks in the embankment.

Claude rammed the throttle. Kitty Hawk zoomed forwards with a surge of power that thrust Claude back in his seat.

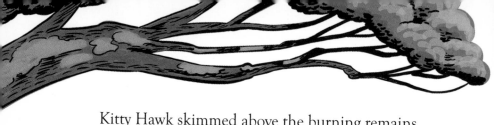

Kitty Hawk skimmed above the burning remains of the tanker, just as the dike gave way. It burst in a wall of white water. The remaining DOGZ soldiers were washed off their feet.

But Claude was away. Soon he was soaring high. With Kitty Hawk's new engine he was quickly out of range from the DOGZ guns. Not that any shots followed him. He glanced back and saw the entire area flooding with water. Sergeant Wolfgang and The Red Setter were all washed up (again), and he spotted Buster, safely out of harm's way, up on the windmill.

With pure luck he'd managed to destroy the main road to the front lines — it would be out of use for months. It was a nice payoff for Rex, Buster and Gertie, who had all risked their lives to get Claude on his way home to Paris.

# CHAPTER 9

Claude landed at CATs HQ. A spiral of smoke still hung in the sky where he had flown a victory corkscrew over the airfield. Nurse Sinja and Mitzi were first on the scene, roaring across the airfield in their ambulance to check that Claude was all right.

'Crikey, mate,' said Syd, squeezing Claude in a fierce bear hug. 'We thought you were a goner that time.'

Commander Snookums patted Claude on the back. 'It's a relief to see you safe and well,' she said.

Major Tom sauntered over with a cocky grin. 'Was just about to launch a rescue mission to save your fur. I can't believe you escaped those DOGZ! Terrible what happened out there, eh chum?'

Wigglebum and Picklepurr came tearing towards Claude and gripped him about the legs.

'Well, that's a first,' laughed Manx, jogging behind. 'You brought a plane back without crashing.'

'No thanks to those dirty DOGZ,' grumbled General Fluffington.

'Well, actually . . .' began Claude. But it was no use trying to tell General Fluffington about The White Paw. He'd have a private word with Commander Snookums. Then he spied something near the Chateau. 'The whole mission was a trap,' said Claude. 'And I think I know who's responsible.'

Claude pushed through the crowd and raced off. Everyone followed as he ran to the Chateau.

Mr Tiddles was sneaking out of the building with a pile of papers under one arm.

'Hold it, you traitor!' yelled Claude, cornering Mr Tiddles against the building. 'I know exactly what you're up to.' He snatched the papers from Mr Tiddles' paws.

General Fluffington and the rest of the cats came puffing up behind. 'What in dogs' name is going on here?' boomed the General.

Claude waved the papers at the crowd. 'Here's our spy,' he said. 'I've been keeping an eye on Mr Tiddles. He's always sneaking about at odd times. Think about it. Who has access to all our secret information? Who wrote The Red Setter report, which led us into that ambush? The General's secretary has been passing our secrets to the DOGZ.'

Claude took a good look at the papers in his hands. '. . . and I . . . hang on. What *is* this?'

'What are you blabbering on about, man?' said

General Fluffington. 'Mr Tiddles is no more a spy than I'm a French manicured poodle.'

Mr Tiddles grabbed back the papers. 'If you must know, it's a script. I got a chorus role in the stage version of Major Tom's autobiography — *High as a Kite, the Musical.*

HIGH AS A KITE
THE MUSICAL

Cast: Major Tom, Celine, The Red Setter, chorus

ACT ONE
"Daddy buy me a plane" — Tom
"Kitten love" — Tom / Celine

ACT TWO
"Tomorrow it's war" — chorus
"Who will save the kittens?" — Celine
"(I'm) Top Cat, get back" — Tom
"Bring him to heel" — DOGZ chorus

ACT THREE
"(I'll be) High as a kite" — Tom
"Fight like cats and dogs" — Tom / Red Setter
"Set me free" (the kennel song) —Tom
"I'm not eating no dog roll" — Tom / Red Setter
"Take that!" — chorus
"High as a kite" (reprise) — Tom / Celine

'I've been sneaking off to rehearsals. I knew you'd all make fun of me, so that's why I tried to keep it secret. If you think I'm a spy, then you've gone as barmy as old C-for.'

'Well . . . ahh . . . yes . . . well, I'm terribly sorry about that,' said Claude, flushing red with embarrassment. He quickly changed the subject. 'Anyway, where *is* old C-for? I really must thank him. His smoke machine saved my life more than once. I don't know what we'd do without his inventions.'

They all looked very sombre.

'What is it?' asked Claude.

'Come and see for yourself,' said Commander Snookums. They led Claude to C-for's workshop.

'It's C-for,' explained Commander Snookums. 'We found his workshop in this terrible mess.'

'That's what it always looks like,' laughed Claude.

'No, this is much worse,' added Manx. 'C-for's been kit-napped by the DOGZ.'

Claude furrowed his brows. He remembered what Rex had told him. DOGZ were kit-napping scientists and engineers to work on their dastardly war machines.

A determined glint sparkled in Claude's eyes. What he *most wanted* was to rescue C-for.

'He may be a crazy old cat, but he's *our* crazy old cat. I'm not going to rest until we have our chief inventor back.'

Donovan Bixley has always loved vintage aeroplanes, and still runs outside when he hears one flying over his studio. Just the sight of an old biplane conjures visions of daring adventures to exotic places. He would most love to take a flight in an iconic World War 1 Fokker Triplane – especially if The Red Setter were at the controls!

Donovan has illustrated over 100 books, published in 31 countries. His books have won many awards and have been number-one bestsellers in New Zealand and Norway.

Find out more about Donovan and his work at www.donovanbixley.com